# GEORGE BUTTERWORTH
## and his music

*George Butterworth: Military Cross and regimental badges.*

# GEORGE BUTTERWORTH
## and his music

A centennial tribute by

## IAN COPLEY

**Thames Publishing**
**14 Barlby Road London W10 6AR**

**To
R.D.C.,
a friend of my youth and
fellow music-lover**

*Printed by Bookmag, Henderson Road, Inverness*

# Contents

# Acknowledgements

My most grateful thanks are due to Dr A J Croft, secretary to the Butterworth Memorial Trust; to Mrs Ursula Vaughan Williams for permission to reproduce copyright material; to Messrs Macmillan Publishers Limited for permission to reproduce a chapter from *London Lavender* by E V Lucas; to the music staff at the Bodleian Library; to the staff of the Vaughan Williams Library at Cecil Sharp House; to the staff of the Commonwealth War Graves Commission at Maidenhead; to the library staff at Brighton Polytechnic for their continued courtesy and help; finally my thanks go to my old friend Max Ray, who typed a fair copy from my manuscript and checked the proofs.

# Formative years

On July 12, 1985, there will be celebrated the centenary of the birth of George Sainton Kaye Butterworth, composer, folk-song and dance collector, and infantry officer. The greater portion of his surviving compositions is still regularly performed, and his works stand on their own feet among the most successful products of the now much despised folk-song school. His war diary and letters are valuable comment on army life, both in training and in action.

In his pamphlet *Sir Alex. K. Butterworth, Ll.B., and Captain G.S.K. Butterworth M.C., B.A. (Belfield Papers, No. 5)*, the author, L M Angus Butterworth, added by way of an appendix a partial family tree-cum-pedigree which draws attention to the widespread scattering of the family and the extent to which they served the community in the Anglican Church, in government, and in legal affairs.

By no means the least interesting member of the clan was George Butterworth's father, Sir Alexander Kaye Butterworth, born in 1854, knighted in 1914, who outlived his soldier son by thirty years, dying in 1946.

Sir Alexander was the son of the Revd George Butterworth and Francis Maria, the younger daughter of John Kaye, Bishop of Lincoln. He was educated at Marlborough and — rather surprisingly — London University. He was called to the Bar and practised in the Middle Temple from 1878 until 1883. In that same year he joined the solicitor's department of the Great Western Railway, going on in 1890/1 as clerk to the Bedfordshire County Council, and returning to railway work as a solicitor to the North Eastern Railway from 1891 until 1906, when he became general manager.

He held a variety of official appointments, both before and after his retirement in 1921. For instance, he was chairman of the Civil Service Arbitration Board from 1917 until 1920, and chairman of the Victoria Park Hospital from 1916 until 1935. Other appointments included the chairmanship of the Pedestrians' Association (1930-39).

In 1884 he married his first wife, Julia Marguerite Wigan, the daughter of a Portishead doctor. She had been a professional singer, and had also composed four songs which were published in 1913, two years after her death. It is, perhaps, not unlikely that their son inherited his musical gifts from her. An early biographer has suggested that she must have been responsible for choosing a unique second name for her son, to reflect her musical interests. Can it be a coincidence that a popular concert violinist of the time was one, Prosper Sainton? The family seems to have divided its time between York and London, where their home was in Frognal Gardens, Hampstead, but it was a York musician, Herr Christian G Padel, who gave their son his first formal music lessons.

R O Morris, who contributed to, and edited, a privately printed 'memoir' of George Butterworth which was intended for family and friends, quoted the words of a York friend with reference to this period: 'I have a clear memory of George as a little boy, independent and thoughtful beyond his years and most interesting to watch'. Morris himself commented that 'these early years in the North were probably not without influence on Butterworth's character for he was temperamentally far more akin to the North than to the South, and although he often delighted to style himself a Cockney, the rugged folk of Yorkshire and Durham, with their downright manners and independence of outlook, were always peculiarly congenial to him, notably throughout the time of his military service'.

When he was nearly eleven he was sent as a boarder to a well-known North Yorkshire preparatory school, Aysgarth, where, besides distinguishing himself in his academic work, his musical prowess continued to blossom. He was school captain during his last two terms, and in 1899 he was entered for an Eton foundation scholarship and delighted his family and friends by coming fourth on the list. Morris quotes from a letter penned by an Aysgarth master of the time: 'It might well be no easy task to draw on one's memory for some account of a particular boy, whose time at his preparatory school ended nearly twenty years ago. But I can vividly recall George. He came to school rather late, obviously accustomed to the society of older people and unversed in school fashions. But he was a clever lad who soon made his way among his fellows, and latterly was one who took the lead and was much looked up to by the younger boys. His undoubted popularity was largely based on his kindness and willing helpfulness to newcomers and those who might for any reason be at a disadvantage. Admiration for his striking musical talents (on occasion he could be left in charge of the organ in chapel) and his prowess at cricket no doubt contributed to the same end. I remember so well going with him to Eton for his scholarship examination and can recall how his sensitive nature responded to the amount of success or failure that he assigned to himself on each paper as we talked it over. He was so anxious to gain his object and so keen to conceal his anxiety. In short he stands out in my recollection as one of the remarkable characters in a long list and I felt sure that he would make his mark in whatever career he decided upon.'

For the next five years he continued his academic and musical education at Eton, the latter under the general direction of Dr C H Lloyd, the Precentor, although he was mainly the pupil of Thomas F Dunhill, Lloyd's assistant. In addition to the piano, his musical studies included counterpoint and composition, and it was under Dunhill's guidance that a violin sonata and an orchestral work — a *Barcarolle* — were composed and subsequently performed, the latter conducted by the composer himself at a College concert in 1903. Neither work has been preserved.

R O Morris commented on these schooldays as follows: 'At Eton he took part with credit in the intellectual, social and athletic life of the school, and the long list of prizes and other honours awarded him during his time at the school testify to the significance of his Eton days'.

From 1904 until 1908 he was an Oxford undergraduate — a Trinity man. His father had aspirations that his only son should follow in the paternal footsteps by embracing a legal career. It was settled that he should read 'Greats' and no one seems to have had any doubts as to his fitness for such a demanding school (*Literae Humaniores*), despite the fact that he had come up as a commoner and not as a scholar.

Once established at Oxford he began to exert a strong influence on the university, and those qualities of leadership that had first manifested themselves at preparatory school stood him in good stead. His musical activities took up both time and energy, and it is scarcely surprising that in the end he only achieved a third class in 'Greats' — having previously gained a second in Moderations during his second year.

The musical friends he made both in and outside the university remained with him for the rest of his life. Among the university friends were Hugh Allen, organist and director of music at New College (and subsequently Heather Professor of Music and director of the Royal College of Music); F B Ellis, music philanthropist and concert promoter, R O Morris of New College, who was to become his first biographer; and Adrian Boult, then a first-year student at Christ Church and later a whole-hearted advocate of his music. His musical friends from outside the university included Vaughan Williams, Cecil Sharp, and C B Rootham of St John's College, Cambridge. With these and many other talented Oxford amateurs he took part in the remarkable series of concerts organised by the Rector of the then remote village of Heyford, so graphically described by Boult in his autobiography.

He was elected president of the Oxford University Music Club, and as Hugh Allen remembered: '. . . he established a reputation for directness of method and brevity of speech. His programmes were unquestionable and progressive, his rulings in business were autocratic but wholesome . . . a fearless debater and hater of cant, he said many things hard to be borne, yet he never made an enemy; for behind a somewhat intolerant manner there was real kindness of heart and a generosity that showed itself in many odd ways'.

Vaughan Williams remembered him thus: 'One of my most

grateful memories of George is connected with my *London Symphony*, indeed I owe its whole idea to him [V W dedicated the work to him — IAC]. I remember very well how the idea originated. He had been sitting with us one evening talking, smoking and playing, (I like to think that it was one of those rare occasions when we persuaded him to play us his beautiful little pianoforte piece, *Firle Beacon*), and at the end of the evening, just as he was getting up to go, he said, in his characteristically abrupt way, "You know, you ought to write a symphony". From that moment the idea of a symphony — a thing which I had always declared I would never attempt — dominated my mind. I showed the sketches to George, bit by bit as they were finished, and it was then that I realised that he possessed, in common with very few composers, a wonderful power of criticism of other men's works and insight into their ideas and motives. I can never feel too grateful to him for all he did for me over this work and his help did not stop short at criticism. When Ellis suggested that my symphony should be produced at one of his concerts I was away from home and unable to revise the score myself, and George, together with Ellis and Francis Toye, undertook to revise it and to make a "short score" from the original — George himself undertook the last movement. [This meant, in fact, reconstructing a score from the band parts, as the original score had been sent to Germany — either to a publisher or a conductor — shortly before the outbreak of war. Butterworth anticipated that it would be lost. It was. — IAC]. There was a passage which troubled him very much, but I could never get him to say exactly what was wrong with it; all he would say was, "It won't do at all". After the performance he at once wrote to tell me that he had changed his mind. He wrote: "A work cannot be a fine one until it is finely played, and it is still possible that . . . may turn out equally well. I really advise you not to alter a note of the symphony until after its second performance. The passages I kicked at didn't bother me at all, because the music as a whole is so definite that a little occasional meandering is pleasant rather than otherwise. As to scoring, I frankly don't understand how it all comes off so well, but it does all sound right, so there's nothing more to be said".'

When Butterworth came down from Oxford he evidently felt himself in something of a dilemma about his future. He had quite abandoned any idea of a career at the bar, and since he felt very strongly that a man should be self-supporting, how to live by music was the question to which some answer must be found. To add to his problems was a strong desire to make composition his main field of musical activity, coupled with the certain knowledge that to live by composition alone was impossible. What supporting activity, then, should he try?

Musical criticism was a possible adjunct, and he joined the music staff of *The Times*, working alongside H C Colles under the aegis of Fuller-Maitland, the paper's chief music critic. He 'found the work uncongenial' — despite the fact that he was noted as possessing 'a surprising breadth and certainty of judgement', and when a teaching post came up at Radley College (a public school not far from Oxford) he accepted it in the hope that teaching might prove less irksome than criticism.

Although it is recorded that he founded a choral society, his year at Radley saw him remembered more as ' a personality' than as 'a musician *per se*'. A Radley master of the time recalls him thus: 'We saw at once that someone quite out of the ordinary had joined us . . . The outstanding quality by which Butterworth will always be remembered was personality. He had extraordinary strength of character: he had opinions and the courage of them. He looked facts straight in the face and said what he thought of them. He was intolerant of narrow-mindedness and inefficiency. He had rough corners and a rugged directness of manner coupled with a gift of keen criticism. Few men can have been worse at making an acquaintance or better at making a friend. When once he decided that he liked you, all reserve vanished and there showed a man with wide interests, wide sympathy and a stout heart . . . In his work he had few opportunities of knowing the boys or of being known by them. Such opportunities as he had he made for himself, and there was a generation of Radlians who grew to know him as an enthusiastic player of games, especially racquets and fives. We felt that we

14

could not keep him long at Radley. His real genius was for music, and he was too big a man to live happily in small surroundings. The cloistered aloofness of school life bored him and its ecclesiasticism jarred. I last met Butterworth on the day he enlisted and I have since met various of his Radley friends. Not one of us was surprised at his brilliant career as a soldier. It was the man through and through — to do what he knew to be his duty and to do it well. That was the stuff he was made of'.

At the end of the summer term of 1910, Butterworth left Radley and entered the Royal College of Music as a student.

Not a few composers, even those with a considerable tally of works behind them, have felt the desirability of strengthening their technical foundations, (Schubert, Satie and Vaughan Williams spring to mind). Butterworth, who still regarded himself as something of a musical amateur, certainly saw such a need in himself, and entered the RCM as a mature student (more mature than most) — studying the organ with Sir Walter Parratt as first study, the piano with Herbert Sharpe as his second study, and theory and composition with Charles Wood. Sir Hubert Parry, the director, observed that he was 'one of those we looked forward to doing something individual and of fine quality' and Wood certainly had a similarly high opinion of his pupil. But the necessity of producing work as it were to order, week by week, he found increasingly frustrating, and he left the College in November 1911.

For the next few years he followed his own inclinations, collecting folk-songs and dances, assisting Cecil Sharp with dance demonstrations, taking part in summer schools and kindred activities. The basic problem as to how he should live was still unresolved and could well have remained so had not an Austrian Archduke been assassinated in a Serbian town, and the First World War become inevitable.

# Character of the happy warrior

From hereon Butterworth's life is well documented. His *War Diary* (August 1914 to July 1916), together with relevant letters home and other matters, was published privately by Sir Alexander Butterworth in his *George Butterworth 1885-1916 (Memorial Volume)* (York and London, 1918). It was an act of paternal piety that ensured posthumous recognition of the greatness of his son's stature as a soldier.

At midnight on Tuesday 4th August 1914, when Great Britain found herself to be in a state of war with Germany, George Butterworth was taking part in a folk-dance school at Stratford-upon-Avon. He wrote home to say '. . . we are keeping on the school at present, because it seems the obvious thing for people to continue their normal existence. There will be plenty of time to think about volunteering after the first enthusiasms have cooled down'. The excitement of the time had already touched him, however, and he allowed himself a moment of exultation on learning that his future step-mother, Dorothea Mavor Ionides, who had been visiting a spa near Wiesbaden, escaped from Germany on the eve of hostilities by the simple expedient of driving across the frontier in a motor-car.

Two weeks later he received an offer of help in obtaining a commission from a family friend. In asking his father to express his gratitude, he nevertheless felt that 'it would be the wrong thing to take advantage of private influence at the present time. Such a policy is always dangerous, and seems to me to be only justifiable when one has complete confidence in being good at the job when one has got it. In this case I have no such confidence . . .'

On August 29 he returned to London, but by this time the black news of the retreat from Mons was beginning to filter through, and he learnt that several friends were going to join the 'Duke of Cornwall's Light Infantry' *en bloc* in the hope of staying together. They did this on September 1, and his diary notes that on that day '. . . over 4,000 joined in London alone, and in the next few days those that came in were probably as many as all those who joined during August. This was partly due to increased activity amongst recruiters, partly to the seriousness of the news from France, which during this week-end looked very bad.'

The following day the group of friends reassembled, with many hundreds of recruits, at Horse Guards Parade and after considerable delay, devoted to the distribution of pay and railway passes, found themselves drafted to the depot at Bodmin in Cornwall:

[We] marched off triumphantly to Charing Cross Underground Station, headed by a brass band and much stimulated by the cheers of the crowd. On arriving at Paddington we were allowed to scatter for lunch, and rallied again for the train to Bodmin at 1-30. We decided unanimously that the transport arrangements were not creditable to the Committee of Railway Managers [Butterworth was, after all, the son of the North Eastern Railway's general manager!] The train was an ordinary one, and the amount of space reserved quite insufficient, many having standing room only. Notwithstanding, the journey down was a hilarious one — beer and singing *ad lib* — it was many days before we were so cheerful again. We had two changes, and did not reach Bodmin till after dark. There we were met by a sergeant and marched up without delay to the Barracks. Our reception there was not encouraging; at the gate we were each presented with one blanket, and told that the sleeping accommodation was already overfull, and that we must do as best we could in the open. Some 20 of us accordingly stationed ourselves under a small group of trees. Food was the next question; although we had been given no opportunity for a meal since Paddington, nothing was provided for us. Luckily, the canteen was open, and by dint of much pushing we managed to secure a tin of corned beef and bottled beer. Considering the situation in which we found ourselves — the night was a distinctly cold one for September — it was not surprising that certain of the rougher specimens partook rather freely. Anyhow the result was the most extraordinary night I ever remember. Few made any attempt to sleep, and those who tried were not given much chance. It so happened that we shared our "pitch" with a rabble from Handsworth, Birmingham — a district which is, I believe, notorious. These worthies kept us supplied with a constant stream of lewdness, mostly of a very monotonous kind; there was one real humorist who made some excellent jokes, but they are scarcely repeatable. At about 2 am. we were joined by several unfortunates who had found their tents already occupied (by lice), and preferred the open air and the wet grass. Altogether, it was a remarkable experience, the most surprising thing about it being the complete absence of any attempt at discipline.

Morning found most of the crowd considerably sobered — not to say depressed. Breakfast was long delayed, and when it came consisted of loaves of bread thrown about indiscriminately, and large dishes of tea (mixed with milk and sugar) one dish to eight men. We eked out this allowance with the remains of last night's supper.

Irritation and futility dominated the first day of military life — endless 'parades' to very little purpose and yet another medical inspection. Conditions at the depot were utterly chaotic because the army was completely unprepared for such a flood-tide of volunteers:

Meals were a great difficulty and . . . conditions were all the worse because recruits had been specially told to bring next to no luggage, as they would receive their full kit directly on reaching the depot, whereas, in fact, many received nothing for days, and even weeks, and thus had absolutely no change of clothing.

In the evening general leave to go out was granted, and there was a lively time in the town. Our party took the opportunity to have a good wash and supper in the best hotel — much to the amusement of an officer who was dining at the next table. Our relations with officers are evidently going to be amusing; in normal circumstances I should be against using our comparative wealth for acquiring luxuries which are denied our comrades, but considering the shortage of supplies of all kinds, there is no alternative.

18

I ought to mention that during the day we were joined by the rest of our company — augmented by an eleventh hour recruit, i.e. E.G. Toye — so that our party now was

P.A. Brown, University Teacher
G. Butterworth
F.B. Ellis, Musician
R.A. Ellis, Engineer and Farmer [brother of F.B. Ellis]
F.H. Keeling, Journalist
R.O. Morris, Musician
E.G. Toye, Musician
R.C. Woodhead, Civil Servant.

For the night we were put into a tent — immune from vermin of the grosser kinds —— and were comparatively comfortable.

On September 4 the group was selected to go with the next detachment to Aldershot, where they were to undergo basic training:

About 500 of us travelled by special train, this time with plenty of room. We were not sorry to leave Bodmin. From Aldershot we marched two miles to Watts Common, and were rather pleased to find we were to be under canvas. On arriving at the camp we were served with tea and decent rations, and put into a tent with two young fellows whom we picked up on the journey — decent boys of the clerk class — by name Watts and Coat; they were subsequently 'recognised' as belonging to the party. We turned in feeling quite happy, convinced that anyhow the most uncomfortable camp in the world would be preferable to dirty and overcrowded barracks.

Rudimentary training commenced and the group soon recognised their place within the military hierarchy:

The man we have most to do with is our platoon sergeant, Edmunds, an excellent fellow, and very patient with his men. We are very lucky to be under him, but as a matter of fact most of the sergeants seem to be nice men, and are doubtless chosen largely on that account.

Our platoon lieutenant, Hammond by name, is the only *young* officer in camp who has had any experience worth speaking of, and there again we are lucky. He also seems to be a good fellow, but of course we are not personally acquainted with him, for it is contrary to military etiquette for an officer to have any except purely official relations with privates; with Sergeant Edmunds we are respectfully familiar!

When we first came here there was a great shortage both of officers and NCO's — the vacancies have been gradually filled. Woodhead and Keeling, having had a little previous training, are now lance-corporals, and the former is our section leader. Major Barnet invited applications for commissions from the members of our party, and Toye put in for one and was promptly accepted. He is now in command of a platoon of B Company. The rest of us, after much consultation, decided that the most important thing for us was to keep our party intact; having arranged to serve together, it would obviously be unfair on those who might be left if some of us became officers — (Toye, having joined at the eleventh hour, was held to be free) — so we told the Major that unless all could have commissions, we would continue as we were; naturally enough, that was considered as equivalent to a refusal.

In the meanwhile there has been a great influx of young lieutenants, most of whom have obviously had little, if any, training; there is one who is drilling in the ranks with us, and who had to be shown how to 'form fours'.

How all this will turn out, heaven only knows; personally I should feel uncomfortable at taking on a responsible job without any proper opportunity of training for it. Toye will be all right, for he is amazingly quick and facile, and full of self-confidence; but I am doubtful about some of the others.

There followed three weeks of drill and parades: each day was filled from six in the morning until the early hours of evening. For a while, these activities were somewhat hampered by the absence of regulation boots and other equipment — no khaki uniforms or overcoats meant that the men had no protection from wet and no proper change of clothes. Every shower of rain meant so many more on the sick list. Here again, those with spare cash were able to supply deficiencies (Butterworth bought himself a mackintosh), but the majority were in a poor way. Provision for sickness was practically non-existent. Serious cases were removed to civilian hospital, but there was no 'Regimental Sick-bay' in which minor ailments could be treated, and sufferers were forced to languish in their tents. When

Roland Ellis contracted a chill, 'his brother lodged a respectful but firm protest, and got permission to remove him to a private room at Aldershot' — where he stayed for two days until fully recovered. A precedent was thus established for the party, and he was shortly followed into private quarters by an ailing R O Morris.

Butterworth found life in the overcrowded tents extremely trying. The actual bulk of bodies took up most of the room, but each man needed space for his rifle and bayonet, clothing, bedding, eating 'irons', and personal odds and ends. 'In fine weather we manage fairly well, as we can expand into the open, but the less said about wet days the better. The effect of 14 wet people huddled together is bad for the temper'. The three daily meals were made from rough fare (for which they were prepared) and although monotonous, they found it reasonably good.

> We are supposed to be able to fill up deficiencies at the regimental canteens, of which there are three, one for beer only, and two for food, tobacco, etc. All of these are very unsatisfactory, being quite insufficiently equipped. The beer is simply not worth fighting for; and there is no other way of getting it. The 'dry' canteens are always running short of everything, and there is no way of getting the cup of hot coffee or cocoa which would be so acceptable at night. For our part, we have formed a habit of going into Farnborough every evening and getting a proper supper, but there are not many who can afford that regularly.

Towards the end of September, the issue of uniforms began in piecemeal fashion and this inhibited Butterworth's approach to one of the more gruelling aspects of an infantryman's training when it made its appearance:

> In the afternoon the battalion, accompanied by a bugle band, went for its first 'route march'; about eight miles along roads. Being one of the few still unprovided with boots, I was obliged to abstain, and did orderly work instead. Each man in the tent is in turn orderly for one day. His duties are (1) To secure the rations; (2) To wash up; (3) To keep the tent in order (more or less). In return for this work, which in present conditions is lengthy, he is excused from all drills.

Training, however, was taking a more practical turn:

> Sharp frost in early morning, followed by a fine, warm day. We are getting on faster with our work now, even if we don't know any of it very thoroughly. In the afternoon the company carried out a sham attack. We advanced in a series of extended lines, alternating rushing forward about 50 yards, and then lying down and firing as fast as possible. Rapid fire is supposed to be the chief asset of English infantry. We have also been practising several movements which are quite new, the result of experience of the present War. These are chiefly defensive measures against sudden attacks by cavalry or artillery . . .
>
> We had our first firing practice, miniature range, 10 rounds each. Our lieutenant performed a remarkable feat, missing the target five times running.

By September 24, Butterworth's confidence in himself as a soldier was beginning to grow:

> The question of commissions has again cropped up; we have all been wavering in our minds about it for some time, and seeing crowds of beardless youths shipped down here as officers has made us rather less satisfied with our position as privates: the climax came when the most incompetent of the lot — who actually had his first lesson in soldiering only a few days ago in the ranks of our platoon — was officially appointed as our platoon officer, in place of Hammond, who is probably going to the front. Within the last few days several of us have been approached from different quarters on the subject of commissions. Only yesterday I had a letter from General Ovens, of North Command, practically offering me a commission in his Brigade, the 68th, stationed at Pirbright, near here; and also asking me to name others of our party.
>
> After some discussion, it was decided that I should follow this up, and propose the names of Morris, Brown, Woodhead and the two Ellises; as we considered it improbable that all would be accepted, I grouped the names in pairs — Morris with myself, Brown and Woodhead together, and the two Ellises together — so that no one should be left alone in the lurch.
>
> The only remaining member of our original party (Keeling) is now a corporal, and prefers in any case to remain in the DCLI

(N.B. — There are no commissions vacant in our battalion).

General Ovens had told me to write to the Brigade Major at Pirbright, but, after consulting the Officers here, we decided that a personal interview would be simpler. Accordingly F B Ellis and myself were given leave to go over to Pirbright in Ellis's motor car, which he has been keeping by permission at Farnborough. We had a memorable afternoon. At Pirbright village we stopped for beer, chiefly for the sake of seeing once again the inside of a country inn, and arrived at the camp of the 68th Brigade at about 4-30. It is a much larger camp than ours, as it houses (!) the whole brigade — 4 battalions; on the other hand, things are obviously less advanced, not a single uniform to be seen. The Brigade Major is the Officer temporarily in charge of the whole camp, and we went off to his tent rather uncertain how to approach so exalted a person. We had no need to be nervous; the sentry, whom we had first to satisfy, turned out to be a seedy Tyne-sider, with a two-days' beard; an intensely comic picture. The Brigade Major himself — though more respectable — was scarcely more formidable; what is familiarly called a 'dug-out'; . . . like everyone else in the camp he was dressed in mufti, and appeared to be very vague on the subject of commissions. One theory of his was that all the second lieutenancies were filled up, but that we could probably become first lieutenants or even captains if we chose! Our interview was very amusing, but would not have satisfied a stickler for military etiquette. We came away with an increased respect for the organisation of the DCLI, and without arriving at any result, for the Brigade Major had no power to nominate us himself, and had received no instructions from General Ovens. He promised to let us know something more definite in a day or two.

The day or two stretched into a week or two and, as basic training continued, the group gradually became more acclimatised to army life. Meanwhile, in France, the Allies had successfully launched a counter-offensive (more by luck than tactical judgement), pushing the German line back over the River Marne and thereby reducing the threat to Paris. A curious shroud of unreality clothed the military preparations in England, however, for on September 26, 1914:

The King visited Aldershot. In the morning the whole of our Division (16 battalions) turned out on the Queen's Parade Ground, and were inspected; i.e., the King and Staff walked once across the lines, and we presented arms — a futile proceeding even from the point of view of ceremonial. Considering the labour involved in getting together 16,000 men, it would surely be possible to do something more with them . . .

One curious effect on the mind of our present life is that it is almost impossible to take any interest in anything outside the camp; the War is merely a distant rumour, and intellectual activity is limited to an occasional game of chess. The continued demand for more recruits causes us all great amusement: in fact, if it were not for the discomfort, and the appearance of names that we know in the casualty lists, Kitchener's Army would seem a colossal joke.

*　　*　　*　　*

Although the offer of commissions for Butterworth and his five friends arrived early in October, the DCLI were reluctant to release such promising material and delayed matters further:

Our Company Commander lodged an objection — trivial as well as inaccurate — on the ground that we had already been offered commissions in the DCLI and refused them. To this we replied that we had not previously being given the opportunity *en bloc*, and had not cared to risk breaking up the party by accepting offers singly.

The situation was a curious one. General Ovens, having once made up his mind, stood by us splendidly. I kept up communications with him by means of Ellis's motor car, which carried messages to and from Bullswater Camp (General Ovens' headquarters at Woking) almost daily, and for a whole week a ridiculous three-cornered correspondence went on. General Ovens would send me what practically amounted to a command to join; this I passed on to the Commanding Officer, who invariably ignored it. Why he was so anxious to keep us I cannot conceive, but I fancy it was just bluff, his only object being to save the face of our company commander by making things as difficult for us as possible.

However, to cut a long story short, one day a more than usually firm message came from the General, we were all called off parade and ordered to report ourselves as soon as possible at our new headquarters. An hour or two later the motor car, supplemented by a taxi, was conveying us and all our belongings to Bullswater Camp . . .

Of our original party of eight, two remained behind — Toye, who had been given a commission, and Keeling, who had been promoted to sergeant, and preferred to stay on.

On arriving at Bullswater we found that matters were far from being settled. The General received us most cordially but explained, with some embarrassment, that he really did not know what to do with us now that he had got us. Owing to the delay, some of the vacancies had been filled up, and the War Office, in fact, pretended that there were none left. This he knew to be an exaggeration, but at the same time he hesitated to take us on then and there without some kind of confirmation from headquarters. In any case it was necessary for us all to go up to London to get uniform and kit, and so it was decided that we were to remain at home until sent for. To anyone who knows how the War Office usually deals with these matters, it will not seem surprising that we were all kept waiting a good many days. I found the delay most demoralising as well as annoying. After five strenuous weeks, the feeling of being absolutely idle, while everyone else was busy, was trying in the extreme. One almost began to share the ordinary civilian anxieties from which soldiers in camp are quite free. Perhaps it was as well for one's intelligence that one's interest in the war and things in general should be revived, and I found that this interest remained with me afterwards, which shows the difference between an Officer's life and the almost purely physical life of the private — at any rate, under Watts Common conditions [i.e. those of the basic training camp] . . .

Another rather depressing feature of London at this time was the darkness of the streets at night — the result, apparently, of an Admiralty order. The idea was to obliterate important landmarks in the event of a Zeppelin raid, but it is difficult to see how this would work, and it certainly did not make things any more cheerful.

Getting uniform, etc., was not difficult; Moss Brothers, Bedford Street, W.C. are wonderful people, and 'their Mr Peter' is especially wonderful — he threw things incontinently on my back, and they just stuck there, and fitted beautifully.

I need not go into details about the tedious settlement of our affairs . . . Our dispositions were as follows:—

| | | |
|---|---|---|
| F B Ellis | ) | 1st Lieutenants |
| R A Ellis | ) | 10th Northumberland Fusiliers |
| Woodhead | ) | 1st Lieutenant |
| | ) | 12th Durham Light Infantry |
| Brown | ) | |
| Morris | ) | 2nd Lieutenants |
| Self | ) | 13th Durham Light Infantry |

Originally we were all appointed 1st Lieutenants, but, as the 13th Durhams seemed to be particularly strong in junior officers, Brown, Morris and self requested to be made seconds.

Butterworth was appointed to command a platoon in 'C' Company, and happily accepted his new responsibilities. The diary chronicles familiar, minor hardships of camp life: dust, marquees that collapse on their occupants in a high wind, mud, cold nights with little protection afforded by the canvas, and the eternal, swamping rain that penetrates everywhere. Although born in London, his early life in York made him sympathetic towards people from the North, and he enjoyed these weeks in training:

> . . . chiefly because of the men with whom I have had to deal — in particular, those whom I have been actually commanding. The enormous difference in the rank and file between this and the DCLI is easily explained:—
> (1)  These men are almost all strictly local, instead of a mix-up of Birmingham, London, etc.
> (2)  They are almost all working men (in my platoon 90% are miners).
> (3)  They are *Northerners*.
> Coming here was exhilarating in much the same way as detraining at Newcastle Station — everyone seemed so very much alive.
> There is no doubt that as raw material our men are wonderfully good — physically strong, mentally alert, and tremendously keen; they do not altogether understand the necessity for strict military discipline, but are very eager to learn their job as quickly as possible. They are also very good fellows indeed, and in short it is a great pleasure to be with them.

26

As to the Officers, it is difficult to form any estimate; except for the Colonel, very few have been in the regular army; a few have seen active service in South Africa or elsewhere, but the large majority have had merely Territorial or OTC experience. This is all that could be expected in the case of the subalterns, and in the 13th we seem to have a very good lot, but the lack of real military experience among the senior officers is a serious draw-back.

In the present state of our training a still greater source of trouble is the inexperience of the NCO's, and here we are distinctly worse off than in the Cornwalls; many of them are merely recruits promoted, and practically none have any of the regular's snap and assurance. Perhaps the greatest surprise I had on arriving was to find that after five weeks training I knew quite as much as my company sergeants; at first this was rather a relief, but now one is beginning to wish for more support; the sergeants and corporals are mostly splendid fellows, but have very little authority . . .

The daily routine is very much the same as in the Cornwalls, about six hours' work, with occasional lectures in the evening. We are progressing, however, very slowly indeed, being very badly off for equipment of all kinds. Our rifles are of an obsolete pattern, and quite useless except for drill purposes. Another serious drawback is the lack of space; there is practically no flat ground for drilling, and very little open country either.

If only we could get going, I am sure we should become efficient very quickly, as the men are very keen and physically quite first-rate.

No doubt the first serious news of heavy casualties in France contributed to this feeling of impatience: whilst the army of recruits were undergoing their rudimentary training, the British regular army was being slaughtered at the first battle of Ypres. By mid-November things must have been serious, for, echoing the events of a later war, Butterworth recorded in his dairy '. . . apparently the authorities were expecting a raid on the coast, and in order to facilitate the emergency transport arrangements, all other movements of troops were temporarily cancelled'. By the end of November the worst was over and the front began to stabilise. The 68th Brigade received their orders to move from

Bullswater Camp into winter quarters at Malplaquet Barracks, Aldershot:

> This was rather an interesting performance, as the whole brigade marched in as a body, 100 yards separating each battalion. Appropriately enough the weather was at its worst — a gale of wind and driving rain. This did not make the job of packing and loading any easier, but by mid-day we were all ready to move off. One got some idea from this of the vast scale on which army transportation has to be worked; a brigade is, of course, a comparatively small body, and we were certainly not over-stocked in any way, but it took something like 100 traction engines and motor lorries to move our stuff. These were ranged along the road in an apparently endless line, and made us feel very important. Owing to the wet we were, of course, unable to strike camp, and a party was left behind to do this as soon as the weather allowed.
>
> After an early dinner had been served, we marched off triumphantly in drenching rain, and so, farewell to Bullswater, and at the other end comfortable barrack rooms, and fires in each!

The comfort of barrack life did not last long however, for within three months the unit was in billets at Ashford, [Middlesex?], soon to be followed by a move to Bramshott, near Liphook in Hampshire. Existence seemed monotonous, and at times Butterworth was tempted to believe that they were not meant to see active service. He nevertheless maintained his interest in the outside world, and in the spring of 1915 he wrote to his father, expressing a typical serviceman's view of civilian behaviour:

> These strikes are a nuisance, and I see there is a small one on the NER [his father's railway company]. Personally I should do three things —
> (1)   Hang (or bayonet) all employers whose profits show an increase on previous year.
> (2)   Imprison for duration of war all who organize cessation of labour in important industries.
> (3)   Make Lord Robert Cecil dictator for duration of war, as being the only man in Parliament who has anything useful to say.

His faith in his own *Northerners* was unabated, however, as he had already recorded in his dairy:

> It is to be hoped that those who grumble at national slackness will make an exception in favour of the working people of Durham County; the large majority of these men have given up good jobs and comfortable homes for the best reasons, and are willing to stand almost anything, if only they are allowed to get out and finish the war.

They were soon to be allowed to do so; by the middle of July, rifles and ammunition had been issued, a musketry course had been completed, and the unit was more or less fully trained and equipped. There had been some changes: General Ovens had been retired as unfit for service abroad and the Colonel in command of Butterworth's battalion had been superannuated. Perhaps this was all for the best — his experience of active service had been gained under Wolseley in the great victory over Arabi Pasha at Tel-el-Kebir in 1882. Butterworth himself had been promoted to full lieutenant and, for nearly a month in the absence of seniors, had been Acting Company Commander. In this country there remained one more important military engagement before departure:

> The first sign of possible business to come was on Thursday, August 19th, when the King came down to review the 23rd Division. Very short notice was given, and several officers who were on leave at the time had to be recalled by wire.
>
> This inspection was rather more interesting than most; the Division had its rendezvous in open country about half way between Guildford and Haslemere — an ideal spot for the purpose. It was certainly a fine sight, and the moment when the King, at the head of his train, galloped into sight through a defile in the hills, was quite thrilling.
>
> However, no one suspected any immediate developments, and the interrupted leave was resumed. But it was not destined to be more than a one-day excursion, for on the evening of Friday, August 20th, orders came that we were to mobilize.
>
> Of course everyone was very excited; one felt that a little of the real thing, after months of sham and boredom, must be a change

for the good. The camp was in uproar most of the night — quite in the old Bullswater style.

However, the actual process of mobilizing, apart from the uncertainty of our movements and destination, was not very exciting. As far as I was concerned, it consisted chiefly in making out lists of kit deficiencies and 'pinching' as much as possible from the quartermaster. We were not able to get away, as the authorities pretended that we might be starting any moment. Eventually we got our orders to march on Wednesday, August 25th. We knew that we were bound for France, but our exact route was not stated, and the censor will not allow me to say anything about it.

At this time in his life music-making must have seemed to be a completely remote activity. We know that the last music of his own he had heard played was his folk-song idyll *The Banks of Green Willow* at an F B Ellis concert on 20th March, 1914. On one of his last leaves, too, he must have looked through his manuscripts, for we are told that before he went to France he destroyed much that he had written, regarding it as unworthy (see Appendix B). His time of music-making was over. By the evening light of August 25, 1915, they set out for France.

*    *    *    *

We had a perfect crossing, by night — getting on and off the boat was a matter of minutes only, and it was impossible to believe it was the work of the War Department. A single destroyer acted as escort, and no incident occurred.

We landed in the early morning and marched a few miles to camp, where we rested for the remainder of the day. In the middle of the night we moved on again, marched a few miles to a railway and then sat down and waited for a train to take us to the front. The transport arrangements at this point were defective, as we had to wait about two hours by the side of the line, during which time some fifty trains must have passed us, mostly empty and returning to base. At length ours turned up — three first class compartments for the officers and cattle trucks for the men, 40 in each. A rumour got about that we were going straight up to the front, but after a few hours' journey the train pulled up at a small wayside station; here we got out, a French interpreter took charge, and we marched five very hot and dusty miles to _____, a village where billets were provided for us.

Here we remained for over a week — about 40 miles from the firing line — and were fairly comfortable, the officers being quartered in farm houses and the men in adjacent barns. We could hear the big guns quite distinctly most days. During this period we went on training exactly as in England, and quickly relapsed into our dull and monotonous habits; in fact things seemed much quieter than at Bramshott, and the only sense of war was provided by the heavy traffic and scorching despatch riders on the main road which led direct to the British Headquarters.

The country here is not unlike England — and the people also. It is possible that they have been unconsciously influenced by the English invasion, and they have certainly been tremendously sobered by the war. This was very striking, in contrast with our people at home; I never heard a soul speak either jestingly or excitedly about future prospects; the French people are certainly going to stand firm. As for the French soldiers, there were none to be seen. The English army fills the whole countryside, and has become part of the normal life — relations with the inhabitants are excellent, but of course there is none of the enthusiasm such as would have greeted us a year ago.

One of my daily tasks is the censoring of men's letters; I have to read them, sign the envelope and then they are franked by the Orderly Room. This becomes irksome after a time, but it is also of great human interest. I don't think I ever before realised the difference between married and single! As to what they say, of course there is very little news — they all seem astonished at finding they can't understand the language, and they all complain because they can't get English cigarettes. Any present of these will be welcome, *but they must be "Woodbines" (1d. a packet)*.

On Monday, September 6th, we moved on — a long march of over 20 miles. For various reasons this exhausted us very much — in fact far more than anything we had ever done, the chief causes being (1) heat, (2) cobbled roads, (3) weight of packs. As regards the last, I ought to say that out here the men carry all their belongings on their backs, and as we have not yet learnt what to throw away the weight is tremendous. At least one in ten fell out, and one can hardly blame them. The weather has been very hot almost all the time so far. On arrival at destination we put up in billets for the night.

Next day, September 7th, we marched again — only 15 miles this time, but weather hotter still. Nearly half the Brigade fell out on the way! This march brought us within five or six miles of the front, and we could hear the rifles cracking quite distinctly. Billets of the usual country type, *i.e.*, farms and barns.

Next day, September 8th, we were inspected by the General Commanding our Army Corps, who kindly informed us what we were supposed to be doing, a subject about which we had all been very much in the dark. He said that we were to go up into the trenches by platoons, for "instructional purposes", 24 hours at a stretch, being attached to the units actually on duty there. We were to do this for four days (two days in and two out), and then retire into safety for further training and finally take up our own positions in the line, in perhaps two or three weeks' time.

So far as can be determined, the Brigade was located in the vicinity of Armentières and Butterworth appears to have led the way in gaining active service experience: by September 11th he records the end of his first 24 hours "instruction" in the trenches, and by the 18th:

We have been in the fire-trenches three times — twenty-four hours at a stretch. This was just a preliminary canter, and we none of us had any real responsibility, merely assisting those already in possession. Naturally enough we were not put into any of the dangerous sections, but it may be of some interest to describe what a normal day on a quiet part of the front is like. The first day we started from a point some miles in rear, and timed our march so as to get up after dark. As we got nearer and twilight set in, the artillery noises grew more and more insistent; ours seemed to predominate, and every gun within miles had its turn at the evening "hate", which is an affair of regular occurrence. As night set in the artillery fire ceased, but the rifles went on cracking continuously with every now and then a splutter of machine guns. We reached the entrance of the communication trench safely; it is about 600 yards long, and as our guide lost his way several times, we spent quite a long time in it; stray bullets were now flying all about, and the explosive sound they cause as they pass overhead was new to most of us; the depth of the trench, however, made things quite safe. At last we filed into the fire-trench, and immediately opposite the entrance I found, to my astonishment, a little wooden shanty, and the officers of the company having dinner; so just at the moment when I felt braced up for a vigorous onslaught on the Hun, I was hauled off to roast beef and beer, while a sergeant posted my men.

Later on I went along the line with the officer of the watch. Every minute or so a flare went up, and then the enemy position was plainly visible, about a quarter of a mile away (the trenches here are really breastworks, built up high with sandbags).

The sentries and snipers on either side exchange compliments pretty frequently, though there is rarely anything to fire at (I have not seen a German yet). In the trench, one is perfectly safe from them; it is the working parties behind who are worried by the stray bullets. And so it goes on all night, and every night; occasionally a machine gun gets on to a target (real or imaginary) and then there is half-a-minute's concentrated fury, after which comparative peace again.

It is extraordinary how soon one gets accustomed to all this rattle. I slept excellently each night I was in, and as I was not on any special duty I was able to get a decent amount of rest.

By day there is very little rifle fire, the sentries are fewer in number and work by periscope; the German snipers make it dangerous for anyone to expose his head above the parapet by day for more than a second or two (even at 500 yards). In this respect they are all over us — and in fact we are still well behind the Hun in all the tricks of trench warfare; as regards machine guns we have pretty well caught up, and our artillery distinctly has superiority.

As far as my platoon was concerned, we had a very quiet time each day we were up; only one shell fell anywhere near us and we have not had anyone hit. Others have not been quite so lucky; one platoon was caught by a machine gun on its way home the very first night (presumably through the guide's fault), and had five wounded. Another lot narrowly escaped destruction by a mine explosion, but the battalion has lost less than twelve wounded altogether and none killed.

So much for our period of instruction; we are now in divisional reserve four miles behind the front, and expect to take up duty in our own allotted section in about a week's time. There is not much excitement here, but we hear the artillery at work practically all the time; usually it is simply a gun or two trying to annoy somebody, but occasionally there is a concentrated "strafe" for half-an-hour or so, and then we all sit up and wonder if someone is trying an attack; and of course there is always a chance that we may be shelled ourselves. But no one minds that.

Back at home the Zeppelins made their first raid on London, and in his letters to the family he remarked that 'such things seem small out here, where the sounds of destruction are audible all day and night'. Nevertheless it seemed to him extraordinary how long he had managed to keep out of the holocaust — although he had been three times up to the front line, he had so far 'seen only one shell burst, and had not seen a single (a) dead man, (b) wounded man, (c) German, or (d) gun'. His luck was to hold. When, on 25th September, 1915, General Sir Douglas Haig threw his 1st Army Corps into the Battle of Loos, Butterworth's unit was in the controversial reserves which the Commander-in-Chief, Field-Marshal Sir John French, kept under his own control. When required, they were too far in the rear to be effective and, as a result, the British losses in the field amounted to over 50,000. By early October the worst was over:

> You will know all about the latest developments. We have been in reserve all the time, and have seen nothing yet, but plenty of moving about . . . Although big things have been happening, I have very little news to give of the last ten days . . . on Saturday, September 25th, as everyone knows, came the big push, preceded by a two days' bombardment, more or less continuous and at times extremely violent. We had known about this for some days before, but all details were kept dark, and even now we know very little more than has appeared in the papers.
>
> As far as our share went, it consisted in being marched hurriedly about between the bivouac and a certain town where we are now billeted (7 miles) — apparently we were being used as corps (not divisional) reserve — ready to assist wherever required.
>
> So far we have not been needed, and for the last few days things have been very quiet along this front; we can only guess at what is happening elsewhere, and what is going to happen.

Throughout October short periods in the trenches alternated

34

with similar periods resting in reserve. Fortunately things were very quiet in the line: 'there seems to be a temporary shortage (or economy) of shell on both sides, which is probably inevitable after the deluge of September 23-25'. They did, however, suffer several casualties, including two officers. Away from the line, the time spent in reserve was enlivened for Butterworth when he was sent on a machine gunnery course. It also gave him time to write longer letters home:

> Since my last communiqué (!) we have had two turns in the trenches and a short rest between; we are now in billets (fairly comfortable), and it is quite uncertain what we are going to do next, or when.
>
> I will try and give some idea of what daily life in the trenches (*i.e.*, ours) is like, so far as is permissible.
>
> In the first place, there are practically no real trenches at all in this part of the country; we are here practically at sea level, and the spade finds water almost at once, hence protection has to be given with barricades of earth and sandbags. The front barricade is continuous all along the line, and behind it — for protection against shell fire — is a conglomeration of passages and cross walls; the geography of these is worthy of the maze at Hampton Court, and in striking contrast to the neat regularity of trenches built for training purposes. (Incidentally I had never seen a breastwork before coming over here).
>
> As these walls have now been standing for nearly a year, they are in need of constant repair; there are enough rats in them to eat up the whole British Army. One advantage of breastworks over trenches is that one can walk about behind them to a depth of about 25 yards without fear of being hit by bullets.
>
> As to our routine — by night we have a good number of sentries watching the front; these are relieved periodically, and the spare men are kept in readiness for emergencies.
>
> By day there are, of course, fewer sentries, and they work entirely by periscope.
>
> Sentry duty is always taken very seriously, no matter how easy the conditions, and a sentry found asleep is automatically sent up for a court-martial.
>
> The difference between day and night conditions is very great. By night, although spasmodic firing is always going on, we have

not had a single man hit, and one could quite happily eat one's supper on the parapet, provided one retired below for one's smoke!

On the other hand, by day it is usually (though not always) extremely dangerous to expose even the top part of one's head for more than two or three seconds. A German sniper, even at 400 yards, can make pretty good practice at a six inch target, and we have already lost an officer and one or two men in that way. Moreover they frequently crawl out at night and take up a position from which by day they can pot away at our parapet without fear of detection. Of course it is the telescopic rifle that does it, and it is curious that the authorities do not think it worth while to put us on an equality in this respect. But in reality this sniping business is more of a nuisance than a danger, as it is quite unnecessary for anyone to expose himself by day, and by night the sniper can do nothing much.

So much for sentry duty — and there is not much else, as far as routine goes. The rest of the men's time is divided up between (a) rest (chiefly by day); (b) carrying supplies up from the dumping ground (which can be done at any time thanks to the communication trenches); (c) repairs (chiefly by night).

As to the Officers, our duties are similar; we take it in turn to be "officer of the watch," which means constantly visiting the sentries, noting incidents of interest, and generally keeping a lookout; at other times there are occasional odd jobs, but otherwise one can rest, and I usually managed to get six hours' sleep out of twenty-four, which is pretty good — boots always on, when asleep. There is a plentiful supply of dug-outs, and one can be quite comfortable. One dug-out serves as a mess-room for the officers of the company, and we have no difficulty in getting up provisions; the men also get their ordinary rations, and so long as the weather is fine (which, curiously enough, has been the case with us so far) all is well.

So much for daily routine. Now for a few incidents, chiefly connected with sorties into "No Man's Land."

(1) On one occasion we decided to attempt "reprisals" against the German snipers; two men were detailed to go out before daybreak, take up a position, annoy the enemy as much as possible during the day, and return as soon as it got dark. We waited anxiously for their return, and eventually

*George Butterworth — from a photograph of a group of folk-dancers.*

*An early portrait by Miss Wigan.*

*A later portrait by Miss Wigan.*

*A collection of family portraits showing Butterworth in childhood, at Eton (Speech Day), at Leeds in 1913, and folk-dancing at Stratford-on-Avon.*

Headquarters 'phoned up that we were to send out a strong search party (of which more anon). This was not successful, and we had given the men up, but in the middle of the next morning, to our great joy, they turned up, having been in the open for 36 hours.

It appears that they crawled close up to the enemy parapet, and accounted for two men during the day; when it got dark they tried to get back, but were cut off (or thought they were) by patrols; so they lay still all night. Next morning they managed to crawl into a ditch, which fortunately led almost up to our lines. For this exploit they are probably getting a DCM.

(2) The Rescue Party — This was a very tame affair. I was put in charge, and perhaps did not take it very seriously, but it seemed to me that we had a very small chance at night time of finding men, presumably wounded, without having some definite idea of where to look for them. However, it was a novel experience, and probably did us good.

We filed out (about 16 strong) by the usual exit, myself in rear, according to instructions. When just clear of our wire everyone suddenly lay down, and at the same time I heard a noise in a tree just to our left. Feeling sure that it was a man I got hold of a bomber, and together we stalked up to the tree. I then challenged softly, and no answer being given, the bomber hurled his bomb, which went off in great style. It struck me afterwards that it was foolish to give ourselves away so early in the proceedings, but I am only narrating this as an example how *not* to conduct a patrol. After satisfying ourselves that there had never been anyone there, we rejoined the others, and I passed up the order to advance. After ten yards crawling everyone lay down again, and this went on for about half-an-hour. By this time I was getting tired — also wet, and as we only had a limited time at our disposal, I decided to go up to the front — instructions notwithstanding — and push on a bit faster; our procedure, moreover, was beginning to strike me as rather ludicrous, as we were strong enough to frighten away any patrol likely to be out. So we went forward about 150 yards without meeting anything, and as time was getting short, I decided to circle round and return by a different route to our starting point. By this time

everyone had acquired a certain degree of confidence —
seeing that not one shot had been fired in our direction — and
the last part of our journey was carried out at a brisk walk,
and without any attempt at concealment. And so ended my
first and (at present) only attempt at night patrolling.

Casualties, nil.

Results, ditto, except some experience and amusement.

By now he was growing worried about the amount of information he was sending home, and his letters were accompanied by warnings of confidentiality. In future he was to be more guarded in his revelations.

As November came on, so did the rain:

We have now had a full fortnight's 'rest', and for myself it has been almost literally rest. I have done practically nothing but eat, sleep and play chess! (No chess in the trenches, because one is glad to sleep all one's spare time.) There is nothing else to do here — no places to go to, the most frightfully dull country imaginable, and any amount of rain.

I am billeted with two other officers in a nice farm house — with beds (!) — and our only discomfort is the MUD. This word may be said pretty well to describe our existence — it is bad enough here and everywhere, but in the trenches there is nothing else (even the water is really liquid mud). My trench coat now has an extra thickness from top to bottom. In short we are getting some idea of what a winter campaign really is . . . one wades to one's bed [in the trenches], and eats one's dinner with water over the ankles, but with waders and four changes of socks I keep fairly dry.

Temporary relief came in the middle of November, however:

I have just been sent on an eight days' course of instruction in bombs — they are gradually training all men and officers. So for the present I am away from the battalion, and away from all danger, except our own clumsiness in bomb-chucking . . . it was rather a farce as far as I was concerned, being really a course for men, not officers. However, I threw a few bombs with fair accuracy (20-25 yards). It is an easy subject to master, especially now that we have at last got the thing standardized — there is practically only one kind used now, and it is a very neat weapon. In a battle the chief difficulty is to organize your parties, and keep them supplied the whole time; at the present stage of things, of course, we practically never use bombs.

About this time he sent home news that his friend Brown, one of the original group who joined the army together and who had subsequently been commissioned with him in the 13th DLI, had been killed in action on November 4th near La Houssoie:

> You will be very sorry to hear that Brown has been killed; he was out in front of the parapet one night, and seems to have lost his way and fallen into an ambuscade; the man with him managed to carry him back — a wonderful performance, as he was under fire most of the way and had to crawl — and he died on the way to the dressing station.

For his bravery 'the man with him', Private Thomas Kenny, was subsequently awarded the Victoria Cross.

The weather turned very cold in the trenches towards the end of the month, but frost was infinitely preferable to wet. The men found it difficult to sleep because of the cold, but the company kept free of frostbite and other trench ills. They had a quiet time and no casualties at all. Butterworth, however, contracted a chill and was in a convalescent home for four days in early December, instead of returning to the front line. That December, Haig slipped into the position of Commander-in-Chief when his superior was recalled to Home Forces (with a Viscountcy). Butterworth, too, went home the following January — but he was on leave for one week only, in order to be present at his father's wedding to the lady whose escape from Germany at the outbreak of war had so delighted him.

He had an uneventful journey back, except for fog in the Channel. This was followed by a day in Boulogne, which he found very expensive. On return to his unit, however, he was promptly despatched to Hazebrucke for a month's signalling course:

> It promises to be interesting, and at any rate novel. Today (the first) I have already learnt to make a clove-hitch knot, mend breaks in cable, Morse alphabet (more or less), and how to run a line across country — all of which seems very remote from the

war, though of course it is part of a very important department.

And towards the end of February:

> The course has been quite enjoyable; it is the first time I have ever
> taken the slightest interest in anything scientific, and I am begin-
> ning to feel quite a practical man. Besides telephone and 'buzzing'
> we have done work at laying cables, mending ditto, also signalling
> with flag, helio, lamp, etc.

As Butterworth was writing this, the first German shell
exploded in the Archbishop's palace at Verdun — the signal for
a mighty battle in the French sector much further south which
was to flare up sporadically over the next four months, until
finally quenched by the threat of an Allied offensive on the
Somme. As he rejoined his battalion it was on the move south in
the first of a series of stages which were to lead it towards that
terrible rendezvous:

> I hope you got my last, saying that I had rejoined the battalion —
> actually before posting it we got orders to move, and were hurried
> off by train to an entirely different part of the front — or rather not
> the front, but a town about 15 miles behind it [Bethune?]. Our
> present function is obscure; apparently we are no longer general
> reserve, because we (i.e., our Division) have been definitely
> attached to a new Army Corps. The idea at present seems to be
> that we are shortly going to take over a definite section of trenches
> in this neighbourhood.
>
> Whatever happens, thank goodness, we have got away from the
> plain. This is a hilly, mining neighbourhood, very like the north of
> England. We are billeted (very comfortably) in a large mining
> village [Marles-les-Mines?], so the men are thoroughly at home;
> in fact the last few days have been about the best rest we have ever
> had.
>
> I told my NCO's yesterday that I thought the next two months
> would see a definite decision (though not the actual finish). It
> seems arithmetically possible for the Germans to make one more
> offensive on the scale of Verdun, but I think that is their limit, and
> when that is over we shall be through with the winter, and a
> combined offensive on all fronts will be practicable. At present we
> are having a renewal of bad weather — heavy snow today.

The rest did not last long: they were soon on the move south to billets at Fresnicourt (?), from whence they took over dry trenches dug deep into chalky soil, which were much safer than those to which they were accustomed (at Souchez, near Vimy Ridge and not far from Loos?). Butterworth says 'there is historic ground on either side.' Towards the middle of March the weather turned fine and warm, and for two months of spring they alternated between periods in the trenches and in reserve. The latter were appreciated: 'away from trenches, at present in a remote country village, full or orchards, birds and streams — manoeuvres all the morning, which at least help to keep one healthy.' Although things in the trenches were moderately lively, they had no serious trouble and as late April turned to May he was able to write:

> It is difficult to realise that we have really come through a winter campaign; I suppose one can consider it satisfactory as a test of physical fitness, though we have certainly been lucky, the worst weather nearly always having found us in billets. We have been equally fortunate as regards the attentions of the enemy, and there must be few battalions with seven months' trench experience whose total killed amount to less than fifty.

He was home on leave from June 1st-8th, his father reporting him in excellent health and spirits. The journey back took 'two whole days, including a night in Boulogne', and when he rejoined his unit it was out of the line. A fortnight later they moved south 'a good long way to a different part of the line' (Amiens?). The push on the Somme was about to begin:

> (July 2nd, 1916). By the time you get this the papers will be full of what is going on here. At present we know very little, except that the much-advertised offensive has started, and made some progress.
>
> We are at present acting as reserve at what seems about the centre of the main push. We have been moving up by easy stages — billets each night — and are at present about 12 miles from the line. Everything seems very quiet, and we can scarcely hear the guns, a phenomenon I completely fail to understand. It is impossi-

ble to say how soon we shall come into action, but we are bound to do so sooner or later, unless our plans go wrong altogether. Fortunately the weather has turned fine, and seems likely to remain so.

(July 3rd). Last night we moved up a bit further, and are now within an easy march of the front. When we got to our destination (at about midnight) we found our billets full of prisoners. So the whole brigade was turned into a field and ordered to bivouac [at Millencourt?]. This consists chiefly in lying down on a waterproof sheet. The men have no overcoats! I have my Reading mackintosh, and managed three hours' sleep — not bad with the temperature little above 40 degrees. There is no mistake about the bombardment now. We get very scanty news from the front, and have seen no papers since the show began. Weather still fine, and pleasantly warm in the daytime.

(July 5th). I'm afraid these letters will reach you very late — the mail is much interrupted and I can't get any field cards. We moved here on the 3rd, about five miles behind the line; bivouacs, but we fortunately have some tarpaulin tents. Last night we were ordered forward, but after we had marched about three miles [to Bécourt Wood?], orders were cancelled, and we returned to our starting point. At least we had the satisfaction of seeing a few (!) of the British guns in action.

We still get very little news — on the whole things seem to be going well, if rather slowly. The French have done brilliantly, as usual, but they probably had the easier job.

From the 7th to the 10th, the British having by that time captured the first system of German trenches, the brigade took part in the second series of operations, of which an attack on Contalmaison formed part. The attack began on the morning of the 7th, but apparently it was not until the 9th that the two battalions of the Durhams succeeded in capturing Bailiff Wood to the west of the village, one of the main objectives of the brigade. On the 11th they were relieved and marched back to Albert. It must have been at this time that Butterworth was forced to take over local command:

I have had charge of my company . . . since the OC was wounded. I was standing beside him at the time, and I think the one shell laid

46

out about a dozen (a very rare event). In fact I must have been the only man in the neighbourhood untouched, and suffered no after effects except slight deafness in one ear, which has now passed off. I tell you this to cheer you up !!

He was to remain in command until his death. For his work during this period he was recommended for the Military Cross, but he made no mention of it in his letters home:

(July 12th — his birthday). In brief my news is
    (1)   We have been up to the front line for a few days.
    (2)   Have done no actual fighting.
    (3)   Are back in rest for a few days.
I am not going to attempt any description — of course the conditions are utterly different from anything we are accustomed to. The ordinary placid routine of trench warfare exists no longer; one had a general sense of confusion, and shells fly about day and night. Add to that wet weather, and mud that requires all one's energy to wade through, and you will have some idea.

All the same it is obvious that our hardships are child's play compared to what the Germans are undergoing — our guns give them no rest whatever.

(July 14th). . . . We were up in the line for a few days, which seemed like so many weeks — but on the whole we had extraordinary luck. We never came into actual close contact with the Hun, but on the other hand we never knew exactly where he was, and often were quite vague as to where we were ourselves. Our worst enemy was the weather, which for two days was really bad. It sounds incredible, but it is true that the mud was far worse than in any of the Armentières trenches throughout the winter. This is chiefly due to the soil. We are now back, billeted in a certain town. I lost practically all my portable equipment, and finally came out with
    1 revolver (unused)
    1 map, and
    1 flask (empty!)

The brigade was then lent to another division which had lost heavily, and on the 15th marched eastwards again to the Tara-Usna line of trenches, the objective this time being Pozières on a gentle ridge astride the Albert-Bapaume road. On the night of the 17th the Durhams made an unsuccessful attack on a German trench, in which one company lost every officer, and, as a frontal attack on the village seemed impracticable, the next two days were occupied in consolidating some 1,600 yards of new trench within 250 yards of the enemy. The brigade was then relieved by the Australians — who eventually captured Pozières six days later. They reached Albert at 4 a.m. on the 20th, and on the same day marched back 10 miles to rejoin their own division, which had been resting near Frenvillers. For his work in this operation Butterworth was once again recommended for, and on this occasion awarded, the Military Cross. The citation reads:

> Lieutenant George S.K. Butterworth. Near Pozières from 17th to 19th July, 1916, commanded the Company, of which his Captain had been wounded, with great ability and coolness. By his energy and total disregard of personal safety he got his men to accomplish a good piece of work in linking up the front line. I have already brought forward this officer's name for his work during the period 7th to 10th July, 1916.

Once again Butterworth tended to minimise his rôle in his letters home:

> We are out again for a rest, and I hope a good one this time. The last was not much use, as we were still within the shell area, and the concussion of our own guns brought portions of the rickety cottages down every time.
> We are now well back, and the noise of battle is only just audible.
> We have now had two turns in the battle line (more or less) and the second was better than the first — at any rate as far as weather was concerned. I will try and write some account of our doings and post it to you at some future time, when the contents will no longer be anathema to the censor.
> We have again been lucky (*i.e.*, our battalion); twice we have been within an ace of being shoved into a desperate venture, but as a fact we have not attacked at all yet — consequently practically all our casualties are from shell fire, and, as you know, only a very small proportion of these are fatal, or even serious.

At Frenvillers the brigade was reorganised and replenished by drafts, but the 'rest' was very short — only five days — for on the 26th they marched from Frenvillers through Contalmaison (which had fallen on the 10th of that month) and joined the right of the Australian Division about half a mile east of Pozières, the dividing line between the two divisions being a trench called 'Munster Alley'. This trench, which ran at right-angles to the British front straight into the enemy's lines, had been repeatedly attacked without success. The day after their arrival the brigade made a fresh attack and secured 70 yards of the trench. Although not involved in the attack, Butterworth sustained a minor wound:

> (July 27th). In the trenches again, at present in support — plans uncertain. No trouble at present except intermittent shrapnel. This morning a small fragment hit me in the back, and made a slight scratch, which I had dressed. This is merely to warn you in case you should see my name in the casualty list! They have a way of reporting even the slightest cases.

They had, indeed! A telegram was received from the War Office reporting him as 'wounded' long before the explanatory letter arrived to allay his parents' fears.

On the night of the 28th the brigade marched back, two battalions to Sausage Valley (south of La Boisselle) and two, including Butterworth's, to Albert:

> Back in billets again after two nights only in the line — nothing much doing. Probably going up again soon.

This short period of rest ended when the brigade was sent to the front line for the fourth (and Butterworth's last) time on the 1st August.

They arrived in a line of trenches situated some 450 yards from the enemy. Here the company was immediately ordered to dig a forward trench from the foot of 'Munster Alley' to a point some 200 yards distant from the German line, so that the brigade could attack with some chance of success. This trench was dug in fog, and was a fine, deep trench which saved many lives in the days to follow. It was called 'Butterworth Trench' on all official maps.

Three days later, on August 4th, the 13th Durham Light Infantry carried out two simultaneous attacks upon 'Munster Alley', one by a bombing party under Butterworth's command, up the trench, and the other an attack 'over the top' from a loop in the trench which bore his name. The latter attack just failed, but the bombing party succeeded in gaining some 100 yards and in blocking the trench not far from their objective, after 'an exceedingly bloody and brilliant attack.'

Brigadier-General H Page Croft, CMG, MP, who commanded 68th Infantry Brigade, went up to the farthest point reached:

> . . . at 4 a.m. in the morning to find the bomb fight still progressing, but the 13th holding their own. Your son was in charge, and the trench was very much blown in and shallow, and I begged him to keep his head down. He was cheery and inspiring his tired men to secure the position which had been won earlier in the night, and I felt that all was well with him there. The Germans had been bombing our wounded, and the men all round him were shooting Germans who showed themselves.

The trench had been so knocked about by bombs and shells that it was low and broken. Some places were very exposed. Soon after dawn on August 5th, 1916, Butterworth was seen by a German, who shot him dead by a bullet through the head. It was within a minute of the Brigadier's departure, who learnt of it by telephone on his return:

> So he who had been so thoughtful for my safety had suffered the fate he had warned me against only a minute before.

Since he was killed in an extremely exposed position only thirty or so yards from the enemy, Butterworth's body could not be brought out to be buried near the Regimental Aid-Post. This was the customary British practice in France because it simplified the problem of later identification. He was therefore buried in a shallow grave close to 'Munster Alley', and the spot was marked with his name and regiment. When the carnage eventually ceased, his body was among those the Army Graves

Service was unable to trace, and for this reason he is commemorated by name on the Memorial at Thiepval, a few kilometres north of the place at which he died.

In writing to commiserate with his father on his loss, the Adjutant of the battalion said:

> He again earned the Cross on the night of his death, and the great regret of the Commanding Officer and all his fellow officers is that your son did not live long enough to know that his pluck and ability as a Company Commander had received some reward.

Throughout his diary and published letters there is no reference whatsoever to musical matters. This, of course, is typical of a man who could devote himself to a single-minded mastery of the art of soldiering when his sense of duty and social background required it of him. It is illustrative of both his unassuming modesty and his purposeful devotion to the task in hand that, after his death, a superior officer could write to his father: 'I did not know he was so very distinguished in music.'

George Butterworth was one casualty in a battle which, between July and October 1916, cost our country 453,238 in killed, or died in hospital, missing, prisoners or wounded. He was killed 24 days after his 31st birthday.

# The growth of musical individuality

Butterworth, whose early works were described by Vaughan Williams as being '. . . hindered and checked, partly by the influence of Schumann and Brahms, and partly by what can be best described as the "Oxford manner" in music — that fear of self-expression which seems to be fostered by academic traditions', is a typical example of a composer whose creative processes were liberated by folk-song and dance.

Ever since the seventeenth century England's instrumental and, to a lesser extent, its vocal music had been composed under the dominant influence of an all pervasive teutonic musical language. Thus, in the late nineteenth century, the teaching of composition by the two most prestigious schools of music in this country manifested this Germanic influence, particularly in the early works of their respective students. Under Stanford's aegis at the Royal College of Music, Brahms was the dominating influence. At the Royal Academy of Music, where Frederick Corder was the chief teacher of composition, a more eclectic Richard Strauss-cum-Wagner style was encouraged.

Particularly after the turn of the century a reaction against this Germanic influence began to appear. There grew a delight in the exotic for its own sake — as in the works of Granville Bantock, which exploited the oriental both in subject matter and, to a lesser extent, in texture. The early works of Cyril Scott similarly demonstrate a repudiation of the teutonic spirit.

The other liberating influence was that of folk-song and dance. It had been Cecil Sharp's hope that there might grow a group of composers who could achieve for English music what the 'mighty handful' had achieved for Russian. Such works as Holst's *Somerset Rhapsody* or Vaughan Williams' *Fantasia on Christmas Carols for baritone solo, chorus and orchestra* exemplify what he had in mind.

The problem was not confined to this country, however. Throughout Europe the 'folk-song-nationalist' composers of the nineteenth century had been handicapped by the basically teutonic idiom that they had inherited. The major/minor key system does not easily fit melodies that are modal in character, and however delightful folk-songs and dances may be, they are not necessarily suitable for symphonic treatment.

The liberation which came about with the dissemination of the works of the French 'Impressionists', especially Debussy, provided the next generation of folk-song-nationalist composers — which included Bartók and Kodaly, for example — with an idiom in which folk-music was naturally at home. Thus, when Butterworth set about clothing the folk-music he had collected in seemly and appropriate settings, this fitting idiom was to hand.

Vaughan Williams recorded: 'It has often been my privilege to hear him improvise harmonies to the tunes which he had collected, bringing out in them a beauty and character which I had not realised when simply looking at them. This was not merely a case of "clever harmonisation"; it meant that the inspiration that led to the original inception of these melodies and that which lay at the root of George's art were one and the same, and that in harmonising folk-tunes or using them in his compositions, he was simply carrying out a process of evolution of which these primitive melodies and his own art are different stages'.

It had been in 1906, while still an undergraduate, that he had joined the English Folk-Song Society and soon became an active member. He collected English folk-music from September of that year until March 1913 (see Appendix 'A') — the songs coming mainly from Sussex, although he also collected in Kent, Hampshire, Herefordshire, Norfolk, Suffolk, Shropshire, Oxfordshire, Berkshire, Buckinghamshire and Yorkshire. The late Lucy Broadwood recorded the following: 'As I write I can see him now, as we first met, when one morning quite early he called here with his arms full of some hundreds (sic) of songs he had collected. He was so eager and so absolutely sincere and so wonderfully gifted'.

Butterworth attended the Stratford-upon-Avon Folk-Dance Summer School in 1911, and later joined the English Folk-Dance Society from its formation in December of that year. He was soon a member of the committee and in 1912/3 was active in helping Cecil Sharp in collecting and editing Morris dances from the Midlands and sword dances from the North. He was one of Sharp's demonstration team members from 1912 until the outbreak of war.

Thus in English folk-music he found the liberating influence for which he had been searching, a source of inspiration most suited to his temperament, and in its study an absorbing activity which coincided with the development of his personal style.

Vaughan Williams further recollected that it was indeed folk-song and dance that provided Butterworth with the means of freedom, enabling him to throw off the fetters that had hindered his earlier efforts, and formed a nucleus that focussed his hitherto vague strivings after those things at which he really aimed. It is certain that his study of folk-song (as scholar, collector and perfomer) coincided with the development of his real musical self.

# The music

As has been related above, Butterworth — while a prep-school boy — was in the habit of sending his mother hymn-tunes which he had written 'away from the piano'. Three of these survive as items in a scrap book which his father later compiled and which is now deposited in the Bodleian library. Although their musical significance is minimal, one of them (the third, in C major) shows some stylistic awareness of the big 'unison' tunes so beloved in school chapels.

The surviving published choral works of Butterworth's maturity consist of two folk-song arrangements and a part-song for female voices and piano. *On Christmas night all Christians sing*, set for SATB (unacc), dates from 1912 and was published that same year. The tune is a variant of the song better known as the *Sussex Carol*, which was collected and arranged by Vaughan Williams. It is a delightful setting and deserves to be more widely popular.

*We get up in the morn* is a traditional English harvest song arranged for TTBB (unacc). It, too, dates from 1912. It was apparently first published that same year by an American firm. Again there is a singular appropriateness of means to ends and it will stand comparison with any similar Vaughan Williams arrangement.

*In the Highlands* is a setting of a poem by Robert Louis Stevenson for female voices (SSC) and piano, and dates similarly from 1912. Although it was written with considerable technical aplomb (his studies with Charles Wood were evidently not wholly wasted), it is much more conventional in texture and could well date from an earlier period of his composing life.

*       *       *       *

Butterworth was an important figure in the post-Victorian development of the English 'art song', and was one of the group of composers who found in that most settable verse of A E Housman a vehicle for their own individual lyric impulses. Arthur Somervell, Vaughan Williams, C W Orr, Ivor Gurney, E J Moeran and John Ireland all set Housman at one time or another, but it was Butterworth in particular who matched Housman's words with an equivalent economy of texture and voice part.

Butterworth's earliest surviving song, however, is a setting of *I fear thy kisses* (Shelley), composed in 1909 and brought out posthumously in 1919, along with a setting of R L Stevenson's *I will make you brooches,* which must have been written about the same time and was published in 1920. From 1910/11 is dated a setting of Oscar Wilde's *Requiescat* which was also published in 1920. Of these settings, *I will make you brooches* will stand comparison with the Vaughan Williams and Peter Warlock settings of the same text. It looks forward to the folk-dominated settings with its all-pervasive flattened sevenths. In the main these early songs are more important as ancestors of the songs of his maturity than as masterpieces in their own right.

In 1911 Butterworth composed his first Housman cycle and at a stroke found himself as a song composer. The *Six Songs from 'A Shropshire Lad'* are studies in economy allied to richness of effect. They range from the lyric beauty of the first song, *Loveliest of Trees* via the light-hearted *When I was one-and-twenty* (the only one that uses real folk material in the melodic line), through *Look not in my eyes* and *Think no more, lad* to the rhythmic subtlety of *The lads in their hundreds* and the stark terrors of *Is my team ploughing?* Ever since their publication in 1911 they have been in constant demand. (It can be noted that the published order of the songs differs from the composer's original order, which was 1 2 3 5 6 4).

A second cycle, *Bredon Hill and other songs from 'A Shropshire Lad'*, was composed in 1912 and brought out the same year. Its opening (title) song, *In summertime on Bredon*, is conceived on a large scale, with an accompaniment which is onomatopoeic beyond his usual fashioning. The setting of *On the idle hill of summer* demands an accompanist of more than average ability to cope with the climax in the last two pages. Had he lived, Butterworth might well have become for Housman what Wolf was for Mörike.

The (eleven) *Folk Songs from Sussex* date from 1912 and were brought out in 1913. There is a short but valuable preface by Butterworth explaining his editorial methods and giving details of the song melodies — who sang them and where, who collected them, and so on. The piano accompaniments have a similar economy and effectiveness to those of the first cycle. He was content to produce simple strophic settings, relying on the vocalists for variety of interpretation.

\*     \*     \*     \*

Between 1900 and 1930 there was among British composers a considerable degree of experiment in the art of song-writing with the voice accompanied by a texture other than that provided by the piano. During this period, before broadcasting had begun sensibly to affect the potential market for 'art songs', conventional song-writing was a fairly remunerative activity for composers. The reasons which occasionally prompted many of them to forsake keyboard accompaniment — which would have ensured the widest currency for their works — in order to grapple with the aesthetic and technical problems of vocal chamber music are of some importance in respect of the overall pattern of musical activity during the first three decades of this century.

Some indication of the extent to which they experimented is to be found in a catalogue — by no means complete — of *Published compositions for a combination of voice with chamber instruments* which appeared in *The Sackbut* for April 1926. This listed some twenty-nine compositions, ranging from single songs to elaborate song-cycles and chamber operas by eighteen British composers.

Among them are: Bantock, *Salve Regina* (string quintet); Boughton, *Five Symbol Songs* (string quartet); Walford Davies, *Six Pastorals* (four solo voices, string quartet and piano); Finzi,

*By Footpath and Stile* (six songs with string quartet); Gurney, *Ludlow and Teme* (seven songs with string quartet and piano); Martin Shaw, *Land of Heart's Desire* (oboe and string quartet); Ethel Smyth, *Four Songs* (flute, violin, viola, 'cello, double bass and percussion); Felix White, *Cradle Song* (string quartet); together with the better known works of Bliss, Holst and Vaughan Williams. Not quoted in the catalogue, but equally worthy of mention, are Butterworth, *Love blows as the wind blows* (string quartet); Gurney, *The Western Playland* (eight songs with string quartet and piano); and Quilter, *Three Pastoral Songs* (piano trio).

Butterworth's contribution to the movement, the cycle *Love blows as the wind blows*, dates from 1914 and was published posthumously in 1921 with a preface by Vaughan Williams (who was Butterworth's musical executor). This cycle of four untitled songs from 'Echoes' by W E Henley has an accompaniment which exists in three versions — for piano, for string quartet and, on hire from its publishers, for small orchestra (flute, oboe, 2 clarinets in B flat, bassoon, horn in F and strings). It should be noted that the small-orchestral version sets only three of the poems, omitting the original No. 3, *Fill a glass of golden wine*. Certainly it can be said that Butterworth has a very noticeable feeling for the orchestra.

Although the Henley cycle was composed after the two Housman cycles, its idiom appears to be less personal in its harmonic language. Despite its technical virtues in the use of unifying thematic material and masterful control of counterpoint, for example, it does not have the immediate impact of the earlier works. In its romantic language one is reminded of certain of the earlier vocal works of Vaughan Williams — in particular the *House of Life* song-cycle, or the cantata *Towards the unknown region*.

\*      \*      \*      \*

In terms of the purely instrumental works, one is immediately aware that Butterworth was deliberately eschewing the symphonic approach. Four of his orchestral works are 'rhapsodic' in form, by which is meant a 'through composed' attitude to structure. Unity is strengthened by the use of thematic 'motifs', and their employment as an element of recapitulation either in terms of key relationships or thematic usage.

The *Two English Idylls (founded on folk tunes)* date from 1910/11 respectively and were published posthumously in 1920. They are scored for normal orchestra less trumpets and trombones (No. 1: 2 flutes, piccolo, 2 oboes, 2 clarinets in B flat, 2 bassoons, 4 horns in F, timps, triangle, harp and strings) (No. 2: 2 flutes, 2 oboes, 2 clarinets in B, 2 bassoons, 4 horns in F, harp and strings). Both Idylls make use of what can be termed a sublimated 'medley' technique, and achieve unity by reason of the delicacy of orchestral sound and variety of textures employed. The first idyll is based on tunes which he himself could have collected, namely 'Dabbling in the dew', 'Just as the tide was flowing' and a version of 'Henry Martin'. The second idyll uses 'Phoebe and the dark-eyed sailor'.

The same observations apply to the third orchestral idyll, *The Banks of Green Willow* (composed in 1913 and also published posthumously in 1918), except that this third idyll uses folk material of the same name — probably collected by Butterworth himself — in a very forthright fashion, though after the main climax the oboe takes up one of the loveliest of all English folk-songs, 'Green Bushes'. It is scored for small orchestra (2 flutes, 2 oboes, 2 clarinets in A, 2 bassoons, 2 horns in F, trumpet in F, harp and strings). In all these works there are Wagnerian harmonies, and the influence of the French Impressionists can be detected here and there.

Of all Butterworth's surviving works, *A Shropshire Lad* (Rhapsody for Orchestra) is the most frequently performed and is the best known and loved. It dates, according to the accepted authorities, from 1912, but the actual composing was spread out over a much longer period of time than that twelve months. Even its title caused problems. It was originally known as *The land of lost content* or *The Cherry Tree* before the present title was arrived at. Its performance by Nikisch in the 1913 Leeds

Festival set the seal on Butterworth's reputation, although it was not actually published until 1917 — a year after his death in action.

Unlike the three idylls, *A Shropshire Lad* does not make use of folk-song, the thematic motifs being derived from the first song (*Loveliest of Trees*) in the first Housman song-cycle. Butterworth added a note to the score to the effect that the work was to be regarded as a postlude or epilogue to both Housman cycles.

It is scored for a large orchestra (2 flutes, 2 oboes, cor anglais, 2 clarinets in B flat, bass clarinet in B flat, 2 bassoons, 4 horns in F, 2 trumpets, 3 trombones, tuba, timps, harp and strings) but the full orchestra is rarely heard, normally he treats the orchestral sound as having the delicacy of chamber music. From the chain of impressionistic thirds (over a pedal) to the miraculously quiet ending, the full structure has the inevitability of genius.

*　　*　　*　　*

The only surviving piece of chamber music is an unfinished suite for string quartet. It dates either from his Oxford days or — and more likely — from his period of study with Charles Wood at the RCM. It is obviously a transitional work, showing acquaintance with the Debussy quartet, especially in the more successful slow movements.

The tally of Butterworth's music is brought to an end with the Morris Dance accompaniments that he arranged. As stated elsewhere, it is not possible to distinguish Butterworth's versions from Cecil Sharp's.

*　　*　　*　　*

## EPILOGUE

It is pointless to speculate as to how Butterworth's compositions would have changed as he grew older. He might have followed the path of Moeran, who became a symphonist in his early middle-age, or he might have followed (or anticipated) Patrick Hadley's solution to the problem of the folk-song symphony. It suffices to keep his memory alive through the performance of his works.

# Appendix 'A'

**COLLECTING ENGLISH FOLK MUSIC**
In his invaluable article 'George Butterworth's Folk Music
Manuscripts' (London: *Folk Music Journal* 1975/9, Vol 3, pp
99-113), Michael Dawney points out that George Butterworth
was one of the most versatile of the early folk-music collectors,
in that he collected, edited, arranged and demonstrated both
folk songs and dances. As a collector he worked either alone, or
with Francis Jekyll (at that time an assistant in the Printed Books
Department of the British Museum), Vaughan Williams or
Cecil Sharp himself. He recorded 460 items, of which 306 were
folk-songs and the remainder dance tunes and step-notations in
various forms. Of the 306 folk-songs, 82 of them were whole and
complete, whilst 174 were tunes lacking only the words. There
were also 10 fragmentary songs and 40 sets of words for which no
tunes were recorded. In round numbers only 50 of these songs
were ever published, the balance remaining in manuscript form
in the collection maintained at Cecil Sharp House.

The collection of folk-music in those days was a colourful
activity. In his delightful entertainment *London Lavender* (London, Macmillan, 1912), E V Lucas painted a fascinating, margi-
nally fictional, account of a collecting session, similar to one
undertaken by Sharp, Butterworth and himself (pp 220-224):

**IN WHICH WE LOSE A FEW CENTURIES AND FIND A
LIVING-PICTURE  BY SIR DAVID WILKIE**
The Director in his search for primitive English music had tidings
of two old Morris dancers in an Oxfordshire village, survivals
from the past when the whole of that county fostered the art, and
he took me to see them. Never have I spent a more curious
evening.

We left the train at Bicester late on a golden afternoon, and
were driven to a little hamlet a few miles distant where the old
fellows lived. They were brothers: one a widower of seventy, still

lissom, and the other a bachelor of sixty-seven, bent and stiff; and with them when we arrived was another elderly man, a little their junior, blowing and beating away at his pipe and tabor as though dear life depended upon it.

Unfamiliar music these instruments give forth, and I defy anyone hearing it to keep his feet still. They are not the drum and fife by any means, although those are the nearest things to them today, nor are they like the old magic drum and pipes of the "Punch and Judy" man (never to be heard again, alas, with a beating heart); but something between the two, with a suggestion of rollick or even madness added. I heard the sounds while we were still approaching the cottage and had no notion what they were; and the strangeness of their melody was increased by the player's total disregard of our entry, although it was a tune that might have ended anywhere. The pipe and tabor have now passed into the limbo of musical archaisms, but it was absurd to allow them to do so. There are certain effects on the stage that no other instruments could so well achieve, and their invitation to the dance is in a simpler way not less commanding than Weber's.

The old fellow played both instruments simultaneously; his left hand at once fingering the three holes of the pipe and supporting the string to which the tabor was suspended, while his right held the little stick with which he unceasingly beat it. For the twain are never separated.

Upon his stopping at last — and I for one could have heard him, uninterfering, for hours — we had a little talk as to his repertory and so forth, until, having changed their boots, the venerable capering brethren were ready. The elder one, Eli, was bright of eye and still very light on his feet; but the younger, Jack, creaked a little. Eli had a gentle smile ever on his curved lips, and as he danced his eyes looked into the past; Jack kept a fixed unseeing gaze on the musician. Together, or alone, they went through several of the old favourites — 'Shepherds' Hey,' 'Maid of the Mill,' 'Old Mother Oxford,' 'Step back,' 'Lumps of Plum-pudding,' 'Green Garters' — and it was strange to sit in that little, flagged Oxfordshire kitchen, with its low ceiling and smoky walls, and watch these simple movements and hear those old tunes. More than strange; for as they continued, and the pipe and tabor continued, I became conscious of a new feeling. For the Morris dance is like nothing else. It is as different from the old English dance as that is different from the steps of the *corps de ballet*. It is the simplest thing there is, the most naïve. Or, if you are in that mood, it is the most stupid; jigging rather than dancing, and very monotonous. But after a little while it begins to cast its spell, in which monotony plays no small part, and one comes in time to hope that nothing will ever happen to interrupt it and force one back into real life again.

The feeling became positively uncanny when old Jack, the bent one, jigging alone, still with his eyes fixed on the musician, but seeing nothing nearer than 1870, began to touch his body here and there in the course of the movements of the dance, every touch having a profound mystical meaning, of which he knew nothing, that probably dated from remotest times, when these very steps were part of a religious or ecstatic celebration of fecundity. Odd sight for a party of twentieth century dilettanti in an Oxfordshire kitchen!

The occasion was not only curious but pathetic too; one saw after a while not these dancers, so old and past the joy of life, but the dancers as once they were, when, forty years ago, they would set out in a team every Whitsuntide, six in all, to dance the Morris in other villages, and sleep in a barn all so jolly, and drink the good ale provided by the farmers, and each strive to be the most agile and untiring for the sake of a pair of pretty Oxfordshire eyes.

Forty years ago!

Asked if there were any others who still remembered the steps, they said no. "We be the last, us be," said Eli, in his soft, melancholy voice. "All the others be dead".

The brothers described, each fortifying the other and helped by the promptings and leading questions of the Director, the ritual of the Morris as they remembered it. A lamb would be led about by a shepherd, and behind this lamb they danced. At night the lamb was killed and the joints distributed. Most was eaten, but portions were buried in the fields. Why, the old men had no notion; they had never heard. But the Director knew, although he did not explain.

For upwards of an hour these energetic enthusiasts continued to dance, sometimes without a hitch, and then again with hesitation and arguments as to the next step or movement. What thoughts were theirs, I wondered. Since he had last danced Eli had married, had had children, had seen his children grow up and his wife die. Yet I am certain that as he skipped and capered on those flagstones in the cottage where he was born, his personality was that rather of a young man than an old. And then the music stopped and he ceased to wave his handkerchief and spring from foot to foot, and he sank into a chair and the light left his face and wistful old age settled over it again.

I congratulated him on his sprightliness, and again asked his age, to make sure.

'Seventy,' he said; 'I shall be seventy-one in July if I live. If I live,' he added, after a while.

'Of course you'll live,' I said, 'You're good for many years yet and many more dances.'

He shook his head.

That he thinks of his end a good deal, I am sure; but never morbidly, or with any affection of sadness, but with the peasant's quiet acceptance of the fact. All his life he has been a tiller of the soil: the same soil, year after year, turning it afresh, sowing it afresh, gathering the harvest afresh, and then beginning all over again — the best school for patience and acceptivity.

And so, after some ale had been brought, we said good-night and drove away, for Oxford and London again, or, in other words, for the twentieth century.

Butterworth's own 'collector's diary' — now in the Vaughan Williams Library at Cecil Sharp House — throws a fascinating light on his ways as a collector, as does the page reproduced with the illustrations (see pp 37-40).

Ursula Vaughan Williams records another incident suggesting that the life of the folk song collector had its occasional hazards (*R.V.W. — a biography of Ralph Vaughan Williams*: London, OUP, 1964):

In December [1911] . . . Ralph went with George Butterworth on a short trip to collect songs in Norfolk. One night, in a pub where they had found several singers, one of them suggested it would be much quicker if he rowed them across the water than that they should bicycle round the Broad by road. It was a brilliantly starry night, frosty and still. They piled their bicycles into the boat and started. Their ferryman rowed with uncertain strokes, raising his oar now and then to point at distant lights, saying 'Lowestoft' or 'Southwold'. Before long they realised they were always the same lights and that he was taking them round and round in circles. The night air after the frowsty bar parlour and the beer had been fatal, and he was thoroughly drunk. Eventually they persuaded him to let them row. Luck guided them to a jetty among the reeds. By this time their singer was sound asleep and did not wake even when they extricated their bicycles from under him. So they tied the boat up and left him there while they bicycled down an unknown track and found their way back to Southwold. The singer survived and was found in the same pub the next evening. But this time they did not accept his offer of a short cut by water.

In all, Butterworth and Vaughan Williams made three collecting expeditions to the Norfolk/Suffolk Broads, in October and December 1910, and in December 1911. Michael Dawney (*op. cit*) tells us that in Butterworth's manuscripts there are copies of 19 songs which they collected together on these trips, and that there are a further 7 songs collected jointly, copies of which appear only in Vaughan William's manuscripts in the British Museum without counterparts in the Butterworth MSS.

Butterworth acted as a co-author with Cecil Sharp of Parts III and IV of *The Country Dance Book* (London: Novello, 1913) and of Part V of *The Morris Book* (London: Novello, 1913). He also arranged a number of Morris tunes for the piano in Part IX and X of *Morris Tunes collected and arranged with pianoforte accompaniment by Cecil J. Sharp and George Butterworth,* (London: Novello, 1913).

We are not told which arrangements are Sharp's and which Butterworth's — and it makes an interesting exercise to differentiate between them on stylistic grounds.

# Appendix 'B'

**COMPOSITIONS LOST OR DESTROYED**

Before Butterworth left for France in 1915 he went through his unpublished MSS and destroyed all those that he felt to be in any way unworthy. From the evidence provided by articles, letters and personal reminiscences, some account of these lost works can be produced.

While still at preparatory school he used to send his mother harmony exercises in the form of hymn tunes, but his real flow of composition began when he became a pupil of Dunhill at Eton. Works first heard there and subsequently destroyed include a string quartet, a violin sonata and a *Barcarolle* for full orchestra.

At Oxford he continued to compose, and the two lost songs *Crown winter with green* and *Haste ye my joys*, both of them settings of Bridges, may well date from his early Oxford days. The piano piece *Firle* (inspired by Firle Beacon, in East Sussex?) was probably produced when he was first discovering and savouring the delicate delights of folk-song.

A more substantial 'lost work' was the *Duo for two pianofortes: Rhapsody on English Folk-songs*, first heard on 20 June, 1910, at an Eton concert, and perhaps the most considerable work to vanish in his self-critical holocaust. It is possible that the incomplete full-score of an *Orchestral Fantasia* preserved in the Bodleian Library derives from this work.

# Appendix 'C'

**SELECT BIBLIOGRAPHY**

ANGUS-BUTTERWORTH, L.M.
  *Sir Alex. K. Butterworth, Ll.B., and Captain G.S.K Butterworth, M.C., B.A. (Belfield Papers, No. 5)*, privately printed, 1979.

BUTTERWORTH, Sir Alexander K. (A.K.B.) (editor)
  *George Butterworth, 1885-1916 (Memorial Volume)*, including a memoir by R O Morris (R.O.M.), privately printed, York and London, 1918.

BARLOW, Michael
  *George Butterworth: the early years*, Journal of The British Music Society, Vol. V, pps 89-100, 1983.

BAYLISS, Stanley
  *George Butterworth, an appreciation*, The Musical Mirror, August 1930, pp. 212 and 228.
  *George Butterworth: 1885-1916*, Musical Opinion, August 1966, pp. 665 and 667.

DAWNEY, Michael
  *George Butterworth's Folk Music Manuscripts*, Folk Music Journal (The English Folk Dance and Song Society), Vol III, No 2, pps. 98-113, 1976.

GRACE, Harvey
  *Butterworth and the Folk Song revival*, The Listener, 1st July, 1942, p. 61.

RIPPIN, John
  *George Butterworth, 1885-1916*, Musical Times, August 1966, pp. 680-682.
  *George Butterworth, Part II*, Musical Times, September 1966, pp. 769-771.

WORTLEY, Russell & DAWNEY, Michael (editors)
  *George Butterworth's Diary of Morris Dance Hunting*, Folk Music Journal (The English Folk Dance and Song Society), Vol III, No 3 pps. 193-207, 1977.

# Appendix 'D'

**CATALOGUE OF EXTANT WORKS**
1   JUVENILIA
*Hymn Tune No. 1.* (A major) (6.6.6.6) (c. 1896-9), setting of unattributed words 'My father, hear my prayer'. Unpublished, Ms in Bodleian Library.
*Hymn Tune No. 2.* (C major) (8.7.8.7) (c. 1896-9), setting of unattributed words 'Hear Thy children, gentle Jesus'. Unpublished, Ms in Bodleian Library.
*Hymn Tune No. 3.* (C major) (8.8.8.3) (c. 1896-9), no words indicated. Unpublished, Ms in Bodleian Library.

2   CHORAL WORKS
*On Christmas Night* (c. 1912). English traditional carol (version sung by Mr Knight, Horsham, April 1907) arranged as a 4-part song, SATB (unacc.) Augener, 1912.
*We get up in the morn* (c. 1912). English traditional harvest song, arranged for TTBB (unacc.) Arthur P Schmidt, Boston, 1912: Augener, 1935.
*In the Highlands* (c. 1912). Words by R.L. Stevenson, arranged for SSC and piano. Arthur P Schmidt, Boston, 1912: Augener, 1930.

3   SONGS
*I fear thy kisses* (c. 1909). Song with piano accompaniment. Words by P B Shelley. Augener, 1919.
*I will make you brooches* (c. 1909/10?). Song with piano accompaniment. Words by R L Stevenson. Augener, 1920.
*Requiescat* (c. 1910/11). Song with piano accompaniment. Words by Oscar Wilde. Augener, 1920.

*Six Songs from 'A Shropshire Lad'* (c. 1911). Songs with piano accompaniment. Words by A.E. Housman. Dedicated to V.A.B.K.

1. *Loveliest of Trees*
2. *When I was one-and-twenty*
3. *Look not in my eyes*
4. *Think no more, lad*
5. *The lads in their hundreds*
6. *Is my team ploughing?*
Augener, 1911.

*Bredon Hill and other songs from 'A Shropshire Lad'* (c. 1912) Songs with piano accompaniment. Words by A E Housman.
1. *Bredon Hill* ('In summertime on Bredon')
2. *Oh fair enough are sky and plain*
3. *When the lad for longing sighs*
4. *On the idle hill of summer*
5. *With rue my heart is laden*
Augener, 1912

*Folk Songs from Sussex.* (c. 1912 — composer's preface dated 30.6.12). Traditional English folk songs with piano accompaniment.
1. *Yonder stands a lovely creature.* Noted by Francis Jekyll. Tune given by Mr Martin, Fletching; Words by Mrs Cranstone, Billingshurst.
2. *A Blacksmith courted me.* Noted by George Butterworth. Tune and words by Mr and Mrs Verrall, Horsham.
3. *Sewing the seeds of love.* Noted by George Butterworth. Tune and words given by Mrs Cranstone, Billingshurst.
4. *A lawyer he went out.* Noted by Francis Jekyll. Tune given by Mrs Verrall, Horsham: Words given partly by her, but chiefly by Mrs Cranstone.

5. *Come my own one.* Noted by George Butterworth. Tune given by the children of Mr Walter Searle, Amberley: words taken from a broadside.
6. *The cuckoo.* Noted by George Butterworth. Tune given by Mr Wix, Billingshurst. The words to which the tune was sung were of inferior quality, and Butterworth substituted

verses given by Mrs Cranstone, Billingshurst.

7. *A brisk young sailor courted me.* Noted by Francis Jekyll. Tune given by Mr Ford, Scaynes Hill; words by Mrs Cranstone.

8. *Seventeen come Sunday.* Noted by George Butterworth. Tune and words given by Mrs Cranstone.

9. *Roving in the dew.* Noted by George Butterworth. Tune and verses 1,4,5 given by Mrs Cranstone; verses 2 and 3 supplied by Vaughan Williams from a version in his possession.

10. *The true lover's farewell.* Noted by George Butterworth. Tune given by Mrs Cranstone; words taken from an old chap-book.

11. *Tarry Trowsers.* Noted by Francis Jekyll. Tune and words given by Mrs Verrall.

Augener, 1913.

*Love blows as the wind blows.* (c. 1914) Cycle of four untitled songs ('In the year that's come and gone, love . . .' 'Life in her creaking shoes goes . . .' 'Fill a glass with golden wine . . .' 'On the way to Kew . . .' Words by W. E. Henley. The music for string quartet, with alternative versions for voice and pianoforte, or voice and orchestra (*fl*, ob, 2 cl in B flat, bsn, hn in F, and str.) Orchestral version sets the first, second and fourth poems only. Novello, 1921. (Preface to published edition by R Vaughan Williams).

4  ORCHESTRAL WORKS

*Two English Idylls (founded on Folk-Tunes)* (c. 1910 and 11 respectively). For orchestra (No. 1: 2 fl, picc, 2 ob. 2 cl in B flat, 2 bsn, 4 hn in F, timps, triangle, hp, and str). (No 2: 2 fl, 2 ob, 2 cl in B, 2 bsn, 4 hn in F, hp, and str)
Stainer & Bell, 1920.

*The Banks of Green Willow.* (c. 1913). Idyll for small orchestra (2 fl, 2 ob, 2 cl in A, 2 bsn, 2 hn in F, tpt in F, hp, and str)
Stainer & Bell, 1918.

*A Shropshire Lad.* (c. 1912) (Originally called 'The Land of lost content', then 'The Cherry Tree (Prelude)') Rhapsody for orchestra (2 fl, 2 ob, cor A., 2 cl in B flat, bass cl in B flat, 2 bsns, 4 hn in F, 2 tpt, 3 tmb, tuba, timps, hp, and str) Novello, 1917.


5   CHAMBER MUSIC
*Suite for String Quartet* (unfinished) (c. 1910?)
Andante con moto, molto espressivo
Scherzando — non allegro
Allegro molto
Molto moderato et expressivo
Unpublished, Ms in Bodleian Library.


6   PIANO
*Morris Dance Tunes.* (c. 1913) Collected from traditional sources and arranged with piano acc. by Cecil J. Sharp and George Butterworth. The tunes were issued in connection with 'The Morris Book,' Part V (by the same authors), which contains a full description of the way in which the dances are performed.
Set IX —
1. *Old Black Joe* (Handkerchief dance: Badby tradition)
2. *The Beaux of London City* (Stick dance: Badby tradition)
3. *The Gallant Hussar* (Handkerchief dance: Bledington tradition)
4. *Trunkles, 2nd version* (Corner dance: Bledington tradition)
5. *William and Nancy* (Handkerchief dance: Bledington tradition)
6. *Leap-Frog* (Handkerchief dance: Bledington tradition)
7. *Lumps of Plum Pudding, 2nd version* (Jig: Bledington tradition)
8. *Ladies Pleasure* (Jig: Bledington tradition)
9. *Helston Furry Dance* (Processional)

Set X —

1. *Bonny Green* (Handkerchief dance: Bucknell tradition)
2. *Room for the Cuckoo* (Handclapping dance: Bucknell tradition)
3. *The Queen's Delight* (Corner dance: Bucknell tradition)
4. *Saturday Night* (Progressive dance: Bucknell tradition)
5. *Bonnets so blue* (Jig: Bucknell tradition)
6. *Constant Billy, 2nd version* (Handkerchief dance: Longborough tradition)
7. Shepherds' Hey, 4th version (Handkerchief dance: Field Town tradition)
8. *Leap Frog, 2nd version* (Handkerchief dance: Field Town tradition)
9. *Wyresdale Greensleeves Dance* (Three-men Dance)
10. *Castleton Garland Dance* (Processional)

Books IX and X of a collection published by Novello, 1913.